WITHDRAWN

E
TEK

Tekavec, Heather
What's that awful smell?

What's That AWFUL Smell?

by Heather Tekavec

illustrated by Margaret Spengler

Dial Books for Young Readers 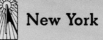 New York

*For Alexandria, the sweet new addition
to our family "farm"*
—H.T.

To my loving mom, Jane
—M.S.

Published by Dial Books for Young Readers
A division of Penguin Young Readers Group
345 Hudson Street · New York, New York 10014
Text copyright © 2004 by Heather Tekavec
Illustrations copyright © 2004 by Margaret Spengler
All rights reserved
Designed by Kimi Weart / Text set in Beton
Manufactured in China on acid-free paper
10 9 8 7 6 5 4 3 2 1

Library of Congress Cataloging-in-Publication Data
Tekavec, Heather, date.
What's that awful smell? / by Heather Tekavec ; illustrated by Margaret Spengler.
p. cm.
Summary: While investigating an odor in their barn, a group of animals
discovers a little piglet and engages in a variety of antics to get rid of the awful smell.
ISBN 0-8037-2660-0
[1 Odors—Fiction. 2. Smell—Fiction. 3. Domestic animals—Fiction. 4. Pigs—Fiction.]
I. Spengler, Margaret, ill. II. Title.
PZ7.T2345 Wh 2004
[E]—dc21   2001054811

The art was created using pastels.

In the middle of a hot afternoon, Dog headed to the barn. He knew it would be cooler in there. He knew there was a meaty bone in there. He knew he could have a quiet nap in there. But he did *not* know what he would find in there.

Dog took one step in and stopped. "What's that AWFUL smell?" he growled.

When Duck arrived a few moments later, he found Dog frantically sniffing around the barn.

"What's going on? What are you doing?" Duck quacked.
Then he choked. "And what's that AWFUL smell?"
"I'm trying to find out," Dog said.

The sheep bounced into the barn next. They stopped and sniffed. "What's that A-A-AWFUL smell?" they bleated.

"Dog's looking," Duck told them.

Soon the cows trudged through the door. They raised their heads and took a deep breath. "What's that AWFUL smell?" they grumbled.

Dog disappeared into the back stall. "Aha!" he barked. "I found it!"

The animals raced to see.

"It's a pig!" they cried.

The little pig made a little oink.

"A pig*let*," Dog corrected. "That's even worse."

"Will it get smellier as it grows?" one cow moaned.

"Yuck, yuck, yuck!" Duck buried his face under his wing.

"It's kind of cute!" a sheep blurted out.

The other animals didn't agree.

"I have an idea," Dog barked. "Get me some hay."

The animals brought great mouthfuls of hay, and Dog covered the piglet from head to toe.

But the smell didn't go away.

The piglet poked its head out from the hay. It looked at Dog.

"Oink," it said.

"What? What? What did it say?" Duck quacked.

"Maybe it wants a ba-a-ath," the sheep guessed.

Dog's eyes lit up. "Maybe a bath would wash away the smell," he said.

"There's a puddle outside," the cows said. "Pigs love puddles."

But this piglet didn't. The animals pushed and pulled, but the piglet wouldn't budge. Finally, Duck jumped in and splashed the piglet instead.

"Oink, oink!" the soggy piglet cried. It ran back into the barn.

And the smell was still there.

"The flowers in our meadow smell good," said a sheep. "Would they help?"

"Let's try," the others agreed, and all the sheep bounded off to get some.

When they returned, the animals spread flowers all over the piglet. They even stuck some in its ears.

But the smell didn't go away.

"Maybe it could live in the chicken coop," the cows suggested. "It already smells bad in there."

"Great idea!" said Dog. Duck nudged the piglet to its feet, and Dog led it to the chicken coop.

But the chickens didn't want the piglet. They cackled when it shook mud on them. They squawked when it curled up in their nest. And when it ate their corn, they chased it right out of the coop.

The squealing piglet ran back into the barn.

And the smell was still there.

"I have one more idea," Dog said. He led them to the strawberry bushes that grew behind the barn. "Nothing smells sweeter than strawberries," Dog said. "Let's put them on the piglet." So the animals carried mouthfuls of juicy red berries back to the barn.

The animals squished berries on the piglet's back. They mashed them on the piglet's legs. They rubbed them on the piglet's snout. When they were finished, the piglet was covered in sticky berries. And so were the animals.

But the smell didn't go away.

"Now wha-a-at?" cried the sheep.

"It will never go away!" moaned the cows.

"Yuck, yuck, yuck!" complained Duck.

"Oink," said the piglet happily as it slurped berry juice off the others.

"I guess there's nothing left to do," Dog said at last.
"We'll just have to stay outside." Dog left the barn.
The cows, the sheep, and Duck followed.
They huddled together in a small patch of shade
until Cat wandered by.

"Why are you all out here?" she meowed.

"There's an awful, smelly piglet in the barn," Dog told her.

"Oh, dear," Cat whimpered. "I hope it didn't eat my dinner."

"Dinner? Dinner? What dinner?" Duck asked.

"My liver, onion, and tuna fish sandwich,"
Cat said. "I hid it in the barn a few days ago."
She strutted inside and the others followed
her to the back stall. From under the hay,
Cat pulled out a fat, squishy sandwich.

"That's the smell!" Dog barked.

"That's her dinner?" mooed the cows.

"It wa-a-asn't the little pig," the sheep bleated.

"Yuck, yuck, yuck!" Duck quacked, and buried his face under his wing.

Cat sniffed the sandwich. "Hmmm," she said.
"It smells kind of rotten. Do any of you want it?"
The animals snorted and backed away.
"Suit yourself," Cat meowed. "I know *someone*
who will like it."

Cat pushed the sandwich in front
of the piglet, who ate it up in one gulp.
"Oink," it said happily.
And the smell was gone.